THE INTERGALACTIC BAND OF BRILLIANCE!

A CRUISE BROTHERS SHORT STORY

CRUISE BROTHERS

RON COLLINS

JEFF COLLINS

SKYFOX
PUBLISHING
Science Fiction

The Intergalactic Band of Brilliance!
A Cruise Brothers Short Story
© 2024 Ron Collins & Jeff Collins
All rights reserved

Songs:
"Theme Song" © Jeff Collins
"Thank You For Trying to Kill Me" © Jeff Collins

Cover Design by Ron Collins
Image: yogysic

Skyfox Publishing

ISBN-10: 1-946176-73-7
ISBN-13: 978-1-946176-73-8

For Robert and Lindsey, and Bob Jr. and Dennis

All the original Cruise Brothers!

THE INTERGALACTIC
BAND OF BRILLIANCE!

oddammit, James, Lyn thought as he bent to pick up the bulky satellite dish. It was a power receiver, and it needed to be properly positioned before the repair could be finished. Only the moon's low gravity — which he hated — allowed Lyn to lift it by himself.

He grimaced with the movement it took to get the dish into position.

Lyn Moore: Service Technician.

Crap.

He'd rather drop into cold vacuum than spend his life working for the boss.

Convinced the alignment was good, Lyn pushed the receiver to snap it hard into place.

"Watch your head!" his co-worker called.

Naturally, it was too late.

The sudden pressure launched him from the floor so fast he did a complete flip and a twist before cracking his skull on the shed's sheet metal ceiling. "Aieee!" The impact came complete with a dramatic boom that split his ears and announced his mistake by echoing through the dingy service tunnels so loudly it drew cackling laughs from every node for a kilo or more.

"Goddammit!" he called, cupping his skull against sharp hot pain.

He fell, slowly, back to the dusty floor.

He twisted like a drunken corkscrew on his way and impacted the ground harder than he expected, scrubbing his hands against coarse lunar concrete when he landed and bruising his knees through the thick black service togs he wore. He hated the uniform. Three interwoven layers of thermal padding under a pressure-resistant layer of what was essentially elastic tin foil.

The suit felt like a plastered-on pajama jumper.

Ugly as sin, and five times heavier.

If I die out there, he'd said to his coworker after putting it on for the first time, *please get me out of this suit.*

He wondered if he'd busted an elbow somehow, but that seemed fine.

At least it moved, anyway. Joy, farking joy.

His cheek was dug so far into the floor he could taste dust. The faint smell of oil from the rig came to him as he rolled to sit up. His eyes watered with pain.

"I hate zero-g," he said.

"I told you not to do that!" his co-worker, a Kadossian named Kashton Jogilla said.

"You most certainly did not!"

Kashton puffed his chest out with something that might have been bravado, or might just have been a false sense of concern that Lyn liked even less than the pain.

"I told you to watch your head," Kashton said.

"Which is most definitely not *don't do that!*"

Standing, Lyn spat floor grime and swung an arm as if to punch the dude — if dude is what Kashton Jogilla was, anyway. Lyn was finding Kadossians — with their bi-jointed legs, their six multi-toned eyes, and their gray-blue skins — hard to define.

He didn't get a lot of that growing up in Casey, Illinois.

The entire species was fun to look at but hard to figure out.

Still, the Kadossian was a pain in the ass. Only the throbbing that still radiated from under Lyn's skull and the fact that he was half a room away kept him from doing some actual punching. That and the fact that he needed to protect his hands.

"The suffering I do for my art," Lyn mumbled to himself.

They had been in the PRCR (Power Receiver Core Room) and disconnected all that clunky spacesuit crap for less than thirty seconds before Lyn decided his co-worker was the most annoying kind of co-worker there was — a real rah-rah Randy, the kind who actually wanted to do a top-flight job rather than just make the power station work again and get the hell out of Dodge.

"*Everyone wants to do a great job!*" the Kadossian had said shortly after they'd started the tram ride to the service order. "*I always pretend I'm at the Universal Service Olympics finals while I'm working,*" he said. "*Always striving to stick that landing! Always looking for a '10' from the Aldebaran judge. How about you?*"

"*Seriously, man, I just wanna gig,*" Lyn had replied

before realizing the alien (to him, anyway) had no clue what he meant by gig. *"I play guitar. That's all. I just wanna rock."*

He was pretty sure Kashton's eyes rolled then, but Lyn had no idea which of the alien's eyes counted when it came to rolling. Kadossians had six, each placed in different regions of the body such that he never knew where to look. The whole thing made him angsty. Which eyes were looking at him? What did they see? A buddy he'd met at the bar last night said Kadossians can see into the personal spectrum. Lyn had no idea what that meant. *"Sounds like a horrible invasion of privacy,"* he'd replied. Which had sounded profound after five or six Lunar ales, but now just worried him even more

"Don't look at me like that," Lyn said, still rubbing a throbbing skull. His head was returning to semi-normal function.

"Don't look at you like what?"

"Just ... just don't look at me."

An awkward silence later, Lyn checked on the dish. At least it was seated. If it was directed properly, the manor of gajillionaire Roscoe Adejeans would soon be receiving a steady beam of the intense photoelectric sizzle juice that it needed to keep the agricultural magnate in lights, oxygen, and other systems in the manner he'd clearly grown to be accustomed to.

Lyn looked at Kashton. "It looks good."

"It's not zero-g," Kashton said, his voice squeaking and four of his eyes now closed as if he was some kind of saint.

"What's that?"

"You said you hate zero-g, but the moon isn't zero-g."

"I don't need science lessons from a Kadossian grunt, Kashton."

His co-worker glanced one eye at the ceiling, now dented with a perfect imprint of Lyn's skull. "I'd say it looks like you do."

Lyn clenched his fist but decided he didn't want to be fired.

Screw it, Lyn thought.

Explaining crap to a Kadossian. He'd hit rock bottom.

"One-sixth g is even worse than zero," he replied. "Too strong for rich morons like Roscoe Adejeans to justify splurging on artificial gravity everywhere, and too low to do any real work in. So, yeah, I hate it. Just like I hate zero-g. Just like I hate this godawful job."

Lyn was too broke to afford mag boots, too, which was the only reason he was working now in the first place — money was tight and, now that he was alone, he needed the cash.

Hence this shit job wearing this shit outfit in next-to-zero g, servicing Adejeans' power systems, and winding up as a machine punch for creating divots in the ceiling.

Life sucked.

As usual, it was his brother's fault.

He and James *should* be laying music down at some gig or recording a new track in their little studio. Banging heads and smashing guitar solos back and forth like the gods they were. That's what they *would* be doing if James hadn't decided to go all hoity-toity and haul his butt off to college.

He was here at Luna U, Lyn grumbled, feeling the pain of knowing his genetically identical twin was so nearby, yet might as well be out in the Aldebaran system for all it mattered.

Intergalactic History, for Hades' sake!

That's what James decided to do with his life.

Intergalactic farking history.

Some opportunity, he thought, remembering James as he sat in their studio after that last session, punching up the idea that he was taking the Luna-U scholarship for the both of them.

I'll be able to make some money, James said. *If I can make a little grub, we can tour like a real band.*

What a wheezer.

Lyn knew James better than James did. Even then he knew his brother was just shamefully afraid of taking a chance. That's where they'd be, though. If James wasn't such a dweeze. If he hadn't caved to the bourgeois idea of a college degree being worth anything. They'd be touring, making sounds, and being what they were supposed to be.

They were the Moore brothers, after all.

The Intergalactic Band of Brilliance.

That's the name James liked, anyway.

Lyn was more set on Middly-Piddly, which he thought was easier to remember and hella more fun to say in front of a throng of fans. *We're Middly-Piddly, my sweet livin' babies, and you're not!*

He just liked how it rolled off his tongue.

Whatever their name, Lyn and James should be stars among stars.

It was only proper. Their destiny. Music was why they'd been born in the first place.

Instead, he was stuck here creating forehead impressions on rich folks' service ceilings.

Lyn glanced at the dent and realized something important. He needed to find a new gig. He was a solo act now, so it wouldn't be as good, but at least it wouldn't be … this.

Goddammit, James, he whispered. *Why'd ya have to go and sell out?*

At least there were enough young grunts in the "colony" that they had a good bar.

He looked at the power grid, still broken, then back to his co-worker, then at the data feed that was processing into his right eye's optical nerve.

Two more hours on the clock.

That meant two more hours till Lunar Ale time and, more important, two hours until the show.

The Feral Sisters were going to perform.

At least there was that to look forward to.

He'd only caught the last few minutes last night before they were whisked off the stage to a smattering of applause and boos that Lyn couldn't understand. In addition to being stunning on the eyes, their whole vibe was yowzah cool. Kind of a rock and roll circus with magic rolled in. Just thinking about them gave him that happy itch that came over him every time he thought something miraculous might happen.

He wanted to see the full act today.

Maybe they'd need a guitar player, he thought. The

idea made him happy. Yes, indeed, maybe they needed a guitar player.

If they did, he was the guy they needed.

"All right, Mr. Universal Service Olympics," Lyn said, finally focusing. He connected the atomizer to the central controller, and turned the amplifier to *full-tilt boogie,* then waved Kashton toward the first stage transformer. "Enough tongue wagging. Get on over there and do your job so we can get the hell out of here on time."

———

"Excuse me," Lyn grunted as he elbowed his way through the narrow, dimly lit, and crowded tunnel. He was close enough to the entrance now that he could just see the flaking airlock bulkhead that was the entrance to the Tap Out — the colony's only legally operating drinking and entertainment establishment of any merit. From ahead, purple and magenta neon lighting flickered over the line of patrons.

It was half past seven and already the place was rocking.

At least there was a pile of folks trying to get in.

Or maybe it was just a line of people trying to breathe fresh air.

Whatever. Ten meters under the lunar surface was no place to dwell on such things.

Lyn was dressed the part, though.

He didn't care about much in life, but he cared about giving a good show — and for his money, giving a good show was all about raw abandon meeting thorough preparation. He could admire that from a million parsecs.

If nothing else, he understood presentation.

Tight trousers with a plated belt buckle that hung low on his hips, a shirt with a skull pattern burned into it — ripped with three diagonal slashes across the belly that were all the thing now — open enough to show a set of rock star abs, and dark enough that he wouldn't blaze like a dweeze when the phosphor black lights kicked in. Its sleeves were three-quarters length, which he preferred because they felt better when he was playing. He had his usual tangle of bangles clattering around his wrists, noting again that he hated how low-g did strange things to them.

He slid past three kids who were decked out in face paint and their own shredded tops.

One, a sallow-cheeked dilly, wore a genetically patched mohawk of neon lime feathers that floated in air currents, her pair of sharp shoulders thrown back against the wall and her leg bent up at an angle, foot pressed on the wall behind her. "Trying too hard, much?" he said to her as he edged past. Her laugh came through her nose. Probably meant to put him down. Made him laugh instead.

Probably a natural-born looney.

Another kid, smoking a vapor wand, exhaled a violet plume of non-carcinogenic breath that caught the tunnel's humid neon flicker as it swirled against the too-low ceiling.

The third was an androgie little git, with motion ink that flowed over their left cheekbone. Leaning back, they gave Lyn an appraising eye and appeared to like what they saw.

"Sorry, Love. Not my type," he explained as he got by.

Eyes on the prize, he thought.

He was here to see the Feral Sisters. If he got in before eight, he'd grab the full act. If he saw the full act, he'd know how he fit in.

Presentation, after all.

He understood presentation, and in this case, it was all about the job.

"Excuse me," he said as he pushed his way to the front of the line. "Paying customer coming through. Excuse me."

"That's the best joke I've heard all day," the robotic bouncer said, its mechanical sensors whining with a hollow tone as its insecty abdomen swiveled to give its claw room to grab Lyn by the collar.

"Hey, watch it with the whiplash, there," he called, twisting to look back at the bulbous brute.

Bash the Bouncer looked to be as much dumpster as it was muscle. Its body was best described as an overly radiated cockroach covered in titanium fiber — or at least something that was supposed to *look* like titanium fiber. Lyn didn't think a place like the Tap Out would spring for the real thing. Its sensors flashed along a ring running around its "head." Metallic screeching came as it moved its collection of eight telescoping arms to fully enclose him.

"Come on, Bash," Lyn said as he held his pay chip high. "I've got cash this time!"

The bouncer scanned the chip like it might be part of

the lost scrolls of Neptune. Its lights flashed a rapid pattern.

"Don't let your circuits boil over there, friend," Lyn said.

"Wonders never end," the robot finally replied with a purposefully mechanical voice, determining the pay was real.

Satisfied, the metallic arm let go of Lyn's collar and he shuffled to collect himself.

"I hate machines," he grumbled as he stepped into the dank stairwell leading to the main floor. Despite sound that already pummeled the tunnel, his footsteps reverberated against the hard metallic stairs — their footpads were worn to bare silver. The walls were as chilled as the rest of the lunar underground, covered in black and blue and plastered with an infinite layer of wildfire graffiti.

Welcome to the Crashbah, read dripping red paint on the wall over the last stair.

A wall of sweetly fragrant body heat hit him as he stepped past that threshold.

Piped-in music nearly threw him against the wall.

The bass was a hammer that nailed his chest with a pulsing drive, percussion threatened to separate his body into its core molecules, and on top of it all, the wail of a synthesized Geiger organ made his senses wobble.

Calling the "Tap-Out" a bar was like calling his Kadossian co-worker a Starfield Scholar.

The Tap Out was a place where young people came to forget they were stuck in a no-place Lunar colony and likely going nowhere they could ever imagine, a place where they could be whoever they wanted to be, where they could be seen, and where they could ogle the whole range of the bar's wildlife while absorbing the heartfelt ambiance of the moment. They came here to unload the days' hard labor, drink a few buckets of equally hard liquor, and maybe dance away a pile of pent-up anxieties before stumbling back through the mind-numbing array of airlocks, jack-tubes, and underground tunnels they called "home" in hopes they made it back well enough they could do it all again tomorrow.

Its owner was an ex-All-Galaxy wrestler named K-Mad-Jenkins, who ran the place with a short fuse and a tight fist. He served as his own bouncer some nights simply because he took legendary joy in tossing out several idiots an hour.

The lighting was dim — just one bare lamplight in the stairwell — its wireframe cage lopsided as if it had been smashed by a baseball bat or some other such flying object. A few more similarly dented cages were spaced around the floor. The smell was rich with alcohol and a mash of bodies from every nook of the galaxy.

The stage was on the far side of the floor, empty of anything but a control board, a collection of musical instruments, and a gathering of wide-rimmed baskets, hoops, and other odd paraphernalia Lyn knew were precursors of what was to come. Three portable holo-projectors formed a triangle at standard points that confirmed the Feral Sisters knew their stuff.

For a moment, he found it offensive that no one else seemed to even notice that the sisters would soon be playing. It made him wonder why a group like theirs was playing a dive like this.

That question was washed away by a wave of relief.

"I'm not late," he said to himself. "Thank the All-Glorious and Ancient Spaghetti Monster."

A pair of bar counters lined the walls both left and right, filled mostly with a milling throng of weirdos and alien workers — a few of which were gyrating out on the "dance pit," the open floor at the center of the place broken by the occasional round table that had been mostly shoved to the side. Torn padding lined the walls along the pit to protect dancers from the smashing they were routinely subjected to.

Dancing was different in low-g.

A young lady spun too hard even as he watched, and half-fell, half floated hard into the fabric.

She picked herself up and kept dancing. No harm no harm.

Lyn breathed it all in.

After his shitty day, nothing was going to kill his joy now.

He threw back his head and sang out an ululating call, then stalked straight to the bar.

"Come to Daddy, baby!" he said, picturing a lunar ale and zeroing in on an open slice of the counter. At least the floor was sticky enough that he didn't need artificial gravity to move.

"When do the sisters play?" Lyn asked the bartender as he got near enough to scream into his ear. It was a human this time, a big guy, clearly with more muscle than brains because otherwise his biceps alone would qualify as genius.

The bartender just stared dolefully back at Lyn.

"Don't do me like that, old chap," Lyn said.

The bartender still did not move.

"I'll have a lunar ale," Lyn added, flashing the pay chip under the pay light. "And when do the sisters play?"

The bartender pulled an ale and set it down. "Pretty much right now," he said, pointing to the stage as random whoops of excitement split the air.

Turning around was a religious experience.

The lighting was still limited, but two shadowed figures strode across the stage like a pair of ballet panthers, each stepping efficiently to check systems, each adjusting a setting here, refocusing a light there.

Just watching brought Lyn a prickle of professional envy.

That the Feral sisters were in full-stop gorgeous mode didn't hurt, either. The dim light accentuated the fact that both were long, curvy, and graceful: The three plagues of the Lyn Moore apocalypse.

Lyn gave a smile of satisfaction.

"Don't get your hopes up little buddy," the bartender said. "They play hard to get."

Lyn's grin steeled as he glanced at the bartender. "Just because *you* couldn't get in their panties doesn't mean they're hard to get."

He picked up his ale and sauntered away before the insult registered.

It boded well that the sisters didn't go for the Chunk-of-Beef kind of guy. That meant they had standards. He liked that ... in an artist, of course.

The ale was sharp at the back of his throat.

He watched as the sisters finished their prep and took positions.

Based on the few minutes he'd caught last night, the Feral sisters' act was an intriguing mix of acrobatics, contortionism, visual theater, and musical interludes. A phenomenon. Something he'd never seen before. A rock and roll circus with a performance art magic show melted into it, which was something he'd never imagined, better yet seen. Maybe that's why the people here didn't seem to get them. The Feral Sisters were too "out there" for the Tap Out.

He glanced around. Not surprising.

Of course, the pair were shapeshifters, too, so maybe that had something to do with it.

Lyn wasn't sure what the term quite meant, but he found it intriguing in more ways than one and he wasn't blind to the way people reacted to the species. Shapeshifters were difficult to accept. Always so fluid, which made them feel somehow … scary.

That they were rare in this sector made them even harder to peg.

He'd looked the sisters up when he got home last night.

Most sources said they were from Shaula, which was a star in the Scorpius system. Of course, there were other origin theories — as there would always be when it came to a pair of shapeshifting creatures from a distant system. Some said they were born from a bottle. Others that they were from a dwarf galaxy far, far away. Others simply said they weren't natural and left it there.

At that thought, a roaring organ riff filled the room.

A smattering of cheers rose through the crowd, and

a raucous voice came over the sound system. *"Ladies, and gentle creatures from around the universe, put your tentacles together and help me welcome to the stage, the Feral Sisters!"*

Light flared.

A tooth-rattling roar of background music blasted.

One of the sisters — keyboard system strapped over her shoulder like a machine gun — launched from stage left, did a languid, looping twist in the air before dropping to a one sharp-kneed superhero pose, all while ripping a piece of music so raw it nearly tore Lyn's spleen straight from his chest, pancreas right behind.

He stood motionlessly. Jaw dropped. Watching.

The intro song became a play in seven verses.

Sister one chameleoned into crimson skin as the rhythm went swooshy, images of war flashed behind her, and new arms appeared where there had been none. A holographic poem wrapped around sister two, who had split her body into parts. (*really*, he thought. *Was that real?*)

More music.

Yes, he said to himself, inserting himself into the mix. *They could use a guitar. There.*

Dance.

And there.

Ventriloquism came to the forefront when sister one brought a pit bro up on the stage and made him say hilarious things over a drumming stream of sound like a free-verse jam.

It was like that forever: a sensation time machine.

Until it wasn't.

When the set finished, Lyn found himself standing

in the same place he'd been when it started, ale now warm in his hand.

———

"You're not their type," said a stocky bruiser when Lyn tried to get to the little round table that the sisters were now sitting at.

Lyn peered up, standing tall as he could and still cradling his mug of ale.

Merc-Sec, he thought. Mercenary security. *Big, dumb, and surly.* The worst kind of security money can buy. Right now, the Merc Sec was doing what he thought his job was, keeping the riffraff from the sisters. It was standard operating procedure for a group touring unfamiliar zones. One can never be too cautious, and Merc Sec was usually cheap everywhere as long as you knew where to look. The mere fact that the sisters had known where to look also spoke to a certain level of professionalism.

Traveling troubadours were a breed of themselves.

"You think I'm a groupie?" Lyn said, blinking innocently.

The bruiser grunted, gave him a bulbous eyeball, then breathed in a breath through his nose. "Looks like a turd, smells like a turd."

Lyn fought the urge to get pissed, which wasn't really that hard. The beef was the beef.

"Get out of here or I rearrange your teeth."

"I admit I like my teeth pretty well where they are," Lyn said, rubbing his jaw.

The bruiser clenched a fist, and muscles flexed all the way to Mare Imbrium.

Lyn waved his pay chip. "I've got a commercial proposition for them. That's all." He waited while the idea fell deeper into the bruiser's skull. "Do you know how pissed they'll be when they hear they missed an opportunity like this simply because of their over-zealous rent-a-goon?"

"Rent-a-goon?"

"So sorry," Lyn waved a dismissive hand. "I meant 'distinguished muscle.'"

"That's better."

"If I can have just ten minutes, I'll see about getting you an in down where I work," he said, noting the place he was under contract with. "It's full-time, and I'm sure they can use a big guy like you to lift up … foundations, or whatever."

"Pays good?"

Lyn waved his chip.

The offer was bogus, of course. No one at SSP would listen to anything Lyn said. The goon didn't need to know that part, though.

"Ten minutes," the bruiser said, tapping his temple with one grubby finger to indicate he was setting the timer on his data feed. "Don't make me come get you."

"Thank you, kind sir." He tipped his glass as he stepped toward the sisters' table.

———

As he drew close, Lyn overheard one of the sisters yell to the other over the speakers. "The gig in Hebron B is next weekend, right?" They were at one of the tenuous little side tables near the stage, a pair of free drinks making rings over the layers of rings that had already been there.

Lyn pulled up a seat and turned it backward before sitting down. Once settled, he put his mug on the table before him.

Sister One gave him the evil eye, then glanced to the bruiser.

The bruiser gave her a cheesy grin and did a fake hat-tip.

"Glorious," she said, sighing and looking at Lyn more closely. "At least you're pretty."

"I'm Lyn Moore," he said.

"Doozie and Fae," Sister Two replied, pointing to herself and then her other half.

She looked at her sister with an expression that left little to the imagination. "He *is* pretty, isn't he?" she said. "Can I keep him?"

"Only if I don't take him home first, Lovey."

He felt a tentacle brush his calf.

Despite himself, Lyn blushed in the darkness.

They were both blonde as he settled deeper into the chair, but then one went purple and pink, and the other did something he'd just agree to call plaid. The closest one then shivered into a silver skin, and then the opposite turned her irises a vibrant green against blue purples at the same time as her lips thinned into something Lyn might have called reptilian if it didn't look so good on her.

He realized then that he couldn't remember which was which.

Doozie and Fae. Fae and Doozie. Yikes. It didn't matter, though. They kept flexing. Red hair one moment, neon branches the next. Sharp chin bones. The fingers of one hand slip-sliding into fleshy appendages that waved as if they were seaweed waving in the open air over the table. Fae (or was it Doozie?) constructed a perky nose, then a pair of nostrils under each cheekbone.

"You like that," Doozie/Fae said when she saw him staring.

"It's a lot more attractive than I would have imagined," he admitted.

There was something about them that made him feel sad, though. Or, not sad, he guessed.

Lonely.

It was James, he realized — watching the sisters riff off each other reminded him his idiot brother wasn't here.

They were twins, after all, connected down to the DNA.

Even though James was a couple of colonies over at the school rather than stashed here in the rubble of Hendrix Station, Lyn had, for example, felt James' presence on the moon when he landed. He'd even debated surprising James, but they hadn't parted well and nothing good could come from that.

Watching Doozie and Fae, or Fae and Doozie, felt

like he was looking in on the kind of shared joke he and James could gear up to without trying.

Despite his excitement at the girls' performance, that loss sent a spear of unhappiness through his heart.

"You're cute," Doozie/Fae said, then turned to her sister. "Seriously? I Wanna keep him."

Unable to wait any longer, Lyn finally blurted: "You two are farking great. Why are you playing in dumps like this?"

Then commenced an awkward moment where Lyn wondered if he'd blown it all.

"I don't know, Darling," Fae/Doozie said, reaching a finger out to run down his jawline. "Maybe we're just slumming between gigs at the Stardust."

He laughed. "As if."

The Stardust Cavern was the biggest gig in the universe — a huge amphitheater dug out of a remote planet that had been designed expressly for the most perfect audio characteristics it was possible to have. The system employed atmospheric reciprocators and audial-shaped scoring to configure mountains and riverbeds in ways that perfected the flow of sound. A concert there reached the entire surface. Any seat on the entire planet had perfect acoustic patterns.

It was every player's dream to appear at the Stardust.

"You *are* great," Lyn said, settling in. "But you need another guitar."

"Oh, really?" Doozie/Fae said, face darkening.

"And if you can't figure out how to play bigger places, you need a manager."

"Like you, I suppose?" Fae/Doozie replied, sipping her drink with a mesmerizing motion.

"Well, yes. The guitar at least. I'd be a shit manager."

"We don't need another guitar."

"Yeah, you do. That bit in the third bar of the … um … spongy song … that was saggy as a dirt umbrella."

The sisters both laughed, glancing at each other as if there was another inside joke going on. He could see he was getting to them, though.

"I'm serious," he said, riding a flare of indignant anger as he relived how the music *should* have gone. "And the next transition was flabby, too. It didn't play at all."

The sister to his left slumped back, staring at him with something that might have been inquisitiveness or might just have been an admiration for his sheer audacity.

"Well, aren't you the cheeky one?"

But her shoulders drooped so far he thought maybe they'd melted, and a fish-like patch of scales suddenly grew over one shoulder.

"Defense mechanism, much?" he said.

The sister hissed.

"Cheeky or not," Lyn said, "we both know you're good enough to know I'm right."

Fish scales glanced at her sister again, and the two shared a cool nod.

"All right," she said. "Show us."

"What do you mean?"

"Right now. Get up there and show us. If we like

what you do, you've got a contract. Otherwise, you can shut the hell up, and we can get onto talking about things we're *all* just a little more interested in, can't we?"

Lyn's face blanched, but he recovered nicely.

He wasn't a hundred percent certain they were saying what he thought they were saying, but the tentacle making its way further north seemed promising.

"That's my kind of offer," he said.

He jumped onto the stage — almost face-planting due to that goddamned lack of gravity.

He grabbed the guitar, strapped it on, and picked a couple of quick chords to remember the song. A power chord turned eyes his way. The house sound fell, leaving him even more attention. He smiled, took one of the big poses he loved so much, and shook out his Now-Too-Short-Because-He-Had-To-Be-Respectable hair.

The bangles on his fretboard wrist twisted against his skin.

The feel of the rounded guitar against his hip and rib cage sent electricity through him.

The crowd gave a razzy cheer.

"Get off the stage!"

"Go home pretty boy!"

He ran his fingers over a quick progression.

"This song already barks!"

Then he plunged into the riff he'd heard inside his head when the sisters had gotten to their soft spot. A moment later he laid an edge down that sliced deep into the piece, bending the rhythm to create padding around his own lead.

Yes, he thought as he caught the melody.

He had been right.

He twisted the beat. Warped the melody with a buzz of the hypnopedal.

A weird holo-sonic effect from the girls' instrument caught him off guard, but he caught it and fed it back into the lead.

This was the place. His place.

He ripped. He poured. He pounded out music, becoming one with the sound — and as he played — he laid his head back to give a primal sound that might have been a wail or a scream or might just have been a raw squeaking of his voice rising into cold, dark space. He felt stars, though. Felt the universe. As he stood on the stage and made his music, he was complete.

Almost, anyway.

His fingers flew over the unfamiliar guitar, learning fast, but there was one hole that would never close. The one James left behind.

He closed his eyes, though.

He closed his eyes and let the music come to him — playing lead over his own rhythm. Fingerpicking, pounding his palm against the guitar's body to get a proper warble.

He breathed deeply.

And then …

Another sound surrounded him. And a feeling … vibrations on the stage and a rhythmic guitar blast that rumbled over the horizon to wash over him, and …

there was a comfortable sensation. A feeling of … completeness.

James?

He opened his eyes.

There he was — his brother, standing on the far side of the stage now, playing another of the sisters' instruments, a crappy little Range-Fire electric that had a throwback sound to it, but playing it like no one but James could have.

Lyn gave a howl and dove into a lead that James fell back on as naturally as if they'd been doing it their whole lives — which, of course, they had. And when James rose up, Lyn left him places to run. In a few moments, people were dancing, or just mashing, bopping heads, and jamming to the free-form piece that seemed to come from nowhere and everywhere at once.

James stepped closer. Lyn leaned in.

Somewhere in there, as they played riff after riff, slowing to a crawl at one point during which Lyn mouthed "how," and James just shrugged, tripped a mic, and screamed "I ain't got the smarts for this shit, baby!" somewhere, the crowd went wild.

———

A half-hour later, with the crowd still yelling for more, the Moore Brothers closed the set.

"Thank you, everyone," Lyn said into the floating mic. He looked over at James. "We're the Intergalactic Band of Brilliance, and — "

"Or Middly-Piddly for short!" James added.

Lyn beamed. "I hope you had a great time, Good Night!"

Then they both flicked their guitar picks into the audience and left the stage.

———

"I think you were right," Doozy said when they clamored off the stage. "We do need another guitar."

Or was it Fae?

Whichever.

Lyn didn't care because he was riding a high as tall as fireworks at the Horsehead Nebula.

"I can't believe you're here?" he said to James as they came to the table.

"Couldn't leave you to screw up the bridge like you always do, now, could I?"

A pair of robobouncers rolled into place to provide security. A set of fresh lunar ales appeared at their table.

"I felt you here, you know?" James said.

"Yeah," Lyn replied. "I know … are you…?" he couldn't bring himself to ask the rest of the question. "Shouldn't you be studying?"

"Let's just say I've given it the old college try and I don't think I'm Intergalactic History material."

Lyn pumped his fist. "The band's back together!"

"Enough of the family reunion," Fae/Doozie broke in. "We need to plan arrangements."

"Arrangements?"

"We have a contract," sister two said. "Remember?"

"I didn't sign anything."

"You voice signed."

"Voice signed?"

"Where we come from a word is a signature."

"Where we come from it most certainly is not!"

"Can you imagine that?" James cut in. "Every politician in the planet would probably self-combust."

"I'd like to see that," Lyn said as an aside, then shook his head.

"So, we leave for Hebron B tomorrow at local 5:00, as they say here. We'll expect you there two hours early." Doozie/Fae said.

"What part of the band's back together again didn't you hear?" Lyn replied.

"Apparently none of it," James replied.

"Which one are you?" Fae asked. Or was it Doozy?

"I'm James."

"No, I'm James," Lyn said. "Two can play at this game."

"I'm not under contract," James said. "I'm not going."

"Whatever." Doozy/Fae shrugged four shoulders. "One of you is more than enough."

"Not happening," Lyn said. "We're the Intergalactic Band of Brilliance!"

"Intergalactic Bob?" Doozy said with a grimace. Or was it Fae? "What kind of name is that?"

"I thought it was Middly-Piddly, Baby," the other replied.

"Like that's any better?"

Lyn took a step back from the conversation, recalling the tantalizing feel of tentacle on leg. He leaned over the table and looked either Doozy or Fae straight in the cheekbone nostril. "I could probably convince my brother to let you sing backup for us if you want to really get together." He waggled a thin eyebrow.

"You've got a better chance of gigging at the Stardust tomorrow, kiddo," whichever sister replied.

"Then I regret to inform you we will be going our separate ways."

"I can't believe you're skipping out on a commitment. Get out of here."

"Oh, Fae," said sister number two, batting a magenta eye at Lyn. "Now that there's two of them, maybe we could just pretend for a day?"

Doozy glared at her sister, then shifted her head to something serpentine and purple. A scent grew caustic.

"I think that's our cue, brother," Lyn said.

"Yeah. Time to ske-daddle," James added. "We need to be making some plans of our own."

The two made their way through the Tap Out, fending off requests for autographs and contact numbers.

"I'm sorry I left like that," James said when they found their way to a quiet place in the corridor leading back to Lyn's cabin. "I just worry about the future, you know?"

"It's all right," Lyn said. "Someone's gotta be the brains."

"True. But I'm better looking than you, too."

"Sadly, no, brother. *I* am the better-looking, smarter brother."

James chuffed, letting it go. It was a bit they had done often enough they could do it in their sleep.

"Intergalactic Bob," he said. "I like that."

Lyn nodded. "Yeah," he said. "Intergalactic Bob. I like it, too."

He grinned then, feeling a sense of momentum building under his wings like he hadn't in too long.

The band was together. There were gigs to chase.

"Yeah, Intergalactic Bob," he said. "I like it."

YOU'VE REACHED
THE END!

We hope you've enjoyed the raucous cruise through the galaxy! If you have, you might find other books in the series to be equally as fun.

Also, if you enjoyed this book, your review on the book retailer of your choice is a great way to help us out. Even a quick line or two can help!

Thank you so much for reading our work!

ACKNOWLEDGMENTS

We would like to thank all the people who have helped us make it this far in life—but, man, that would be a nearly infinite list. Instead, let's narrow it a little. Thanks to all the sets of Collins brothers who came before us. Thanks to Dad, especially, for hanging around while we were brainstorming a bit.

Thanks, too, to Kristine Kathryn Rush, Dean Wesley Smith, and Lisa Silverthorne for throwing their own ideas at us when we asked for a bit of advice. That was a fun lunch.

Thanks to our beta readers, Sharon Bass and John Bodin. You two are the bestest.

Thanks, also, to Karen and Lisa for not laughing at us when we decided to take a flier at this silliness—with special focus on Lisa for being our last reader!

And, finally, thanks to the many airplanes that flew over our recording studio as we were grabbing the audio version of this book. Or, um, actually, no thanks there. Those planes were a real pain.

ABOUT RON & JEFF COLLINS

Jeff and Ron Collins—the original Cruise Brothers—first played music together as youthful teens down in the basement of their home in Louisville, Kentucky. (*"No grass, but a lotta grapes!"* - inside Mom joke, there). While occasionally annoying the family and their beloved cat Frisky with boisterous songs at 2am, there were some gems that have managed to stand the test of time (a few even found their way into this Cruise Brothers series).

Then Jeff fiddled around with theater and improv comedy before hightailing it out to Los Angeles to become a rock star, and Ron found his way through engineering and into the life of a high-powered icon in the science fiction field.

Or something like that.

Now here they are. Back, better than ever.

Aside from composing and producing original works, these days you can find Jeff playing live with several tribute bands, including a tribute to Genesis (Gabble Ratchet), Alice Cooper (Pretties For You), and Jane's Addiction (Jane's Addicted).

Ron's short fiction has received a Writers of the Future prize and a CompuServe HOMer Award. His short story "The White Game" was nominated for the Short Mystery Fiction Society's 2016 Derringer Award.

With his daughter, Brigid, he edited the anthology *Face the Strange.*

You can follow Ron at his website: Typosphere.com
Or join Ron's Readers and get two free books!
typosphere.com / newsletter /

ALSO BY RON COLLINS

<u>Novels</u>

Stealing the Sun (9 books)

Saga of the God-Touched Mage (8 books)

Fairies & Fastballs w/Brigid Collins (3 books)

The PEBA Diaries (2 books)

The Knight Deception

Wakers

<u>Collections</u>

Holiday Hope

They Came Back

Collins Creek (Vol 1) Contemporary Currents and Historical Eddies

Collins Creek (Vol 2) Streams of Speculation

Collins Creek (Vol 3) Tides of Adventure

Tomorrow in All the Worlds

Picasso's Cat & Other Stories

Five Magics

<u>Novella</u>

The Bridge to Fae Realm

<u>Poetry</u>

Five Seven Five (100 SF Haiku)

www.ingramcontent.com/pod-product-compliance
Lightning Source LLC
Chambersburg PA
CBHW030908200726
48289CB00003B/944